Autumn
Publishing

Published in 2019
by Autumn Publishing
Cottage Farm
Sywell
NN6 0BJ
www.igloobooks.com

Autumn is an imprint of Bonnier Publishing

Stories based on the Marvel comic book series *Spider-Man.*

The Story of Spider-Man adapted by Alexandra West. Illustrated by Simone Buonfantino.
A Very Strange Night adapted by Rachel Poloski. Illustrated by Roberto DiSalvo.
The Widow's Sting written by Jim McCann. Illustrated by Roberto DiSalvo.
Mysterio's Revenge adapted by Alexandra West. Illustrated by Aurelio Mazzara and Gaetano Petrigno.
The Swashbuckling Spider written by Arie Kaplan. Illustrated by Simone Buonfantino.
The Hunt for Black Panther written by Jordan Lurie. Illustrated by Aurelio Mazzara and Gaetano Petrigno.
Seeing Spots written by Jim McCann. Illustrated by Simone Buonfantino.
The Amazing Incredible Spider-Hulk written by Arie Kaplan. Illustrated by Simone Buonfantino.
Mega Meltdown written by Jordan Lurie. Illustrated by Aurelio Mazzara and
Gaetano Petrigno.
All stories painted by Tommaso Moscardin, Ekaterina Myshalova
and Davide Mastrolonardo.

0719 001.01
2 4 6 8 10 9 7 5 3 1
ISBN 978-1-78905-960-1

Printed and manufactured in China

MARVEL
SPIDER-MAN
STORYBOOK
COLLECTION

Autumn
Publishing

Contents

MARVEL
SPIDER-MAN
STORYBOOK
COLLECTION

Autumn
Publishing

Contents

MARVEL SPIDER-MAN

The Story of Spider-Man

Peter Parker was just your average teenager from Queens, New York. He lived with his Aunt May and Uncle Ben, and he attended Midtown High School. Peter was very studious and was considered one of the smartest kids in school. Unfortunately, his good grades didn't make him very popular with some of his classmates.

Flash Thompson, the school bully, regularly tormented Peter. One day, Flash pushed him to the ground and Peter's books and papers scattered everywhere. "Hey, Parker, you dropped your books," Flash sneered.

School was tough for Peter, but he was always happy at home. Aunt May and Uncle Ben loved Peter completely. Uncle Ben always reminded Peter that he was going to do something special with his life.

"You are incredibly smart, Peter," Aunt May said. "You have the ability to be anything you want to be."

"Well, actually, I was thinking that I might want to be a scientist some day," Peter replied.

Uncle Ben put his arm round Peter. "Being a scientist is a very important job. Science is power. And remember – with great power comes great responsibility."

Then, one day, Peter's life changed while he was on a school trip to the Science Hall. He was excited to see real-life scientists at work. But while Peter looked around at the exhibits, a spider passed through radioactive waves. Peter was so distracted, he didn't even notice the radioactive spider head right towards him.

At that moment, the radioactive spider bit Peter!
He could never have imagined what an impact
this one bite would have on his life.

Peter Parker would never be the same.

Before Peter knew it, he had adopted many
characteristics of a spider.

He could cling to walls, he was super-strong
and he also had spider-sense. This meant that
Peter experienced a strong tingling feeling that
alerted him to danger. These skills made Peter
extremely powerful.

Peter wanted to keep his identity a secret, so he stayed up all night creating a spider-suit and mask. He even stitched a large spider on the front of it.

Peter also worked hard to figure out how to control his new powers. Using his vast knowledge of science, he made web-shooters and practised shooting them in his bedroom. Peter's super-strong webs stuck to every surface. Soon, his entire room was covered in webs!

Okay, so it's not as easy as it looks, Peter thought.

To make some money, Peter became a wrestler. "Please welcome to the ring... Spider-Man!" the announcer would boom.

Peter used his powers to defeat every opponent.

One night, the wrestling gym was burgled. Peter didn't care and let the robber get away.

Later that night, when Peter got home, he saw police cars in front of his house. He raced inside and found out that someone had attacked and hurt Uncle Ben. Aunt May and Peter were devastated.

The police officers told Peter not to worry because they had the criminal cornered at an old warehouse. But Peter knew he had to take matters into his own hands.

Peter put on his Spider-Man suit and swung through the city.

He was determined to avenge Uncle Ben.

Spider-Man arrived at the warehouse. He shot a web and trapped the crook. After getting a good look at him, Spider-Man realised that it was the same criminal he had let escape from the wrestling gym.

If only I had stopped him then! he thought. Peter vowed that from then on he would help others whenever it was in his power.

Just one month earlier, Peter would have been busy studying for his chemistry exam like any normal teenager, but everything had changed. He might still have to do homework from time to time, but Peter was also Spider-Man.

The next day at school, everyone couldn't stop talking about Spider-Man.

"I think he's great," Flash said, as he looked at an article about the new hero. "He's just trying to help the city."

Peter smiled. If only Flash knew who Spider-Man really was!

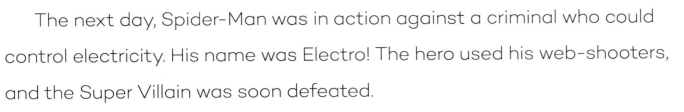

The next day, Spider-Man was in action against a criminal who could control electricity. His name was Electro! The hero used his web-shooters, and the Super Villain was soon defeated.

In that moment, Spider-Man thought back to what Uncle Ben had told him – with great power comes great responsibility. He now knew it was his destiny to protect others.

Peter Parker might seem like your normal teenager, but there is a part of him that is extremely special. He is a Super Hero who can scale buildings and spin webs.

He is the Amazing Spider-Man!

MARVEL
SPIDER-MAN
A Very Strange Night

Spider-Man has been called many things: amazing, spectacular and sensational. But today, no matter how hard Peter Parker tried, he wasn't feeling amazing, spectacular or sensational.

Today, Spider-Man was very, very sleepy. For the last week, Peter hadn't slept through the night.

His dreams were troubling, silly and sometimes downright spooky. A week of nightmares makes for one sleepy crime-fighter.

Peter didn't think much of it, until one very long spider-yawn almost allowed Shocker to ruin the Policeman's Ball! Spider-Man groggily swung into action. He webbed Shocker's gauntlets before knocking the vibrating villain to the floor with a well-timed kick.

"Look! Not only is he a menace, but Spider-Man was sleeping on the job!" shouted J. Jonah Jameson from his table as Spider-Man swung away.

Spidey knew he needed to see a specialist, someone who was truly an expert on dreams and the human mind. And he knew just the doctor to call.

Doctor Strange explained that he knew all about Spider-Man's sleepless nights. "The Eye of Agamotto has shown me that you've been experiencing nightmares," Strange told Peter.

"And now it will show those nightmares to me."

Soon, Doctor Strange was looking at Spider-Man's nightmares. In some, he was back in elementary school and forgot to wear his trousers. In others, the Sinister Six were winning every battle against him. Doctor Strange was not only able to see the future and the past — he could also see right into a man's very soul.

A Very Strange Night

"Your sleep is interrupted by the supernatural, your dreams are being invaded by the most dastardly of nocturnal threats – your mind is plagued by the villainous Nightmare himself!" Strange shouted.

With a snap of his fingers, Strange placed Peter into a deep trance. Then, with the help of the Eye of Agamotto, he dived straight into Peter's dreams.

Peter once again found himself in front of his entire class without his trousers on. Though he was embarrassed, he was no longer alone. Doctor Strange stood tall beside him, urging him to see the nightmare for what it truly was.

Peter concentrated and the class vanished. They were replaced by the master of bad dreams, Nightmare, and his trusty steed, Dreamstalker!

"The Sorcerer Supreme commands you to release your hold on this hero!" shouted Strange. But Nightmare simply laughed.

"I take power from dreams, Doctor Strange," Nightmare began, "and with a hero as strong as Spider-Man, I'll finally be great enough to defeat you!"

As Doctor Strange and Nightmare launched into combat, Peter knew he had to help the Sorcerer Supreme. Even in the dream state, Spider-Man had to lend a hand! He realised he knew just how to do it – by using the power of imagination!

Peter thought and thought and thought, as hard as he could. To his amazement, the dream around him began to change! They weren't in Peter's school any more, but on a giant chessboard, and Spider-Man was in control of the pieces!

"It would seem Spider-Man is using the powers of his own dreams against you!" Doctor Strange declared to Nightmare.

Spidey played move after move, defeating Nightmare's pieces, until the villain was the only one left in play. Outnumbered, the villain retreated, leaving Peter's mind.

"You've won today, Strange, but you've not seen the last of me!" Nightmare shouted as he rode Dreamstalker out of Peter's mind and back to his home in the shadow realm.

"Don't worry, I look forward to defeating you again," Doctor Strange replied.

Peter woke with a start, pleased to find the good Doctor waiting with a hot cup of tea. "This is Wong's special herbal blend," Doctor Strange said. "It should calm your mind after a night like this."

A Very Strange Night

After saying goodbye to his old friend, the tired hero swung home, changed into his pyjamas and slipped under the sheets. There were no monsters under the bed, and the only things in his wardrobe were his clothes and his spider-suits.

So, for the first time in what felt like weeks, Peter Parker finally got an amazing night's sleep.

MARVEL
SPIDER-MAN
The Widow's Sting

Spider-Man was casually swinging through the streets of New York City. It was the weekend, and crime-fighting had been kind of quiet, not that he was complaining. Sometimes a Super Hero could use a nice day of just wall-crawling and web-slinging.

Looking down, he thought he saw a familiar face in the shadows.

He swung over to take a closer look.

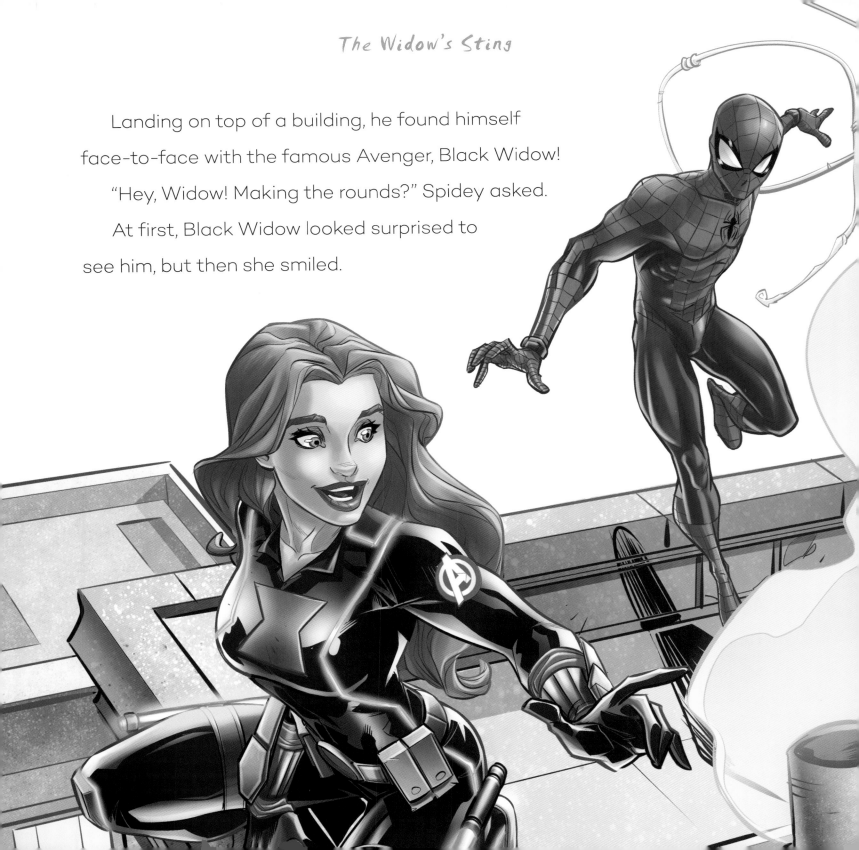

Landing on top of a building, he found himself face-to-face with the famous Avenger, Black Widow! "Hey, Widow! Making the rounds?" Spidey asked. At first, Black Widow looked surprised to see him, but then she smiled.

Spider-Man noticed she was staring at something. He followed her gaze to Avengers Tower in the distance. "If you're looking to head home soon, I could give you a ride," he offered. "Spidey-style."

Black Widow's smile grew. "Yes, it would be wonderful to see the Avengers again."

Again? Spidey thought. **Black Widow is an Avenger. Wouldn't she be there all the time?** But Spider-Man, not being an Avenger himself, shrugged it off.

Black Widow climbed onto Spider-Man's back. "Hold on," he said as they swung towards Avengers Tower.

When they arrived at the tower, Spider-Man walked up to the security door and placed his hand on the scanner.

"Avengers Guest, Spider-Man. Identity: Confirmed. Welcome," the computerized voice said.

"What a friendly building," Spidey noted.

The doors opened and Spider-Man began to walk inside.

Black Widow started to follow, but Spider-Man stopped her. "Don't you have to check in?"

Black Widow lifted her cold eyes. Spider-Man's spider-sense tingled.

"Of course," Black Widow said, placing her hand on the security scanner.

The alarm began to sound. "Identity unknown. Intruder alert! Intruder alert!"

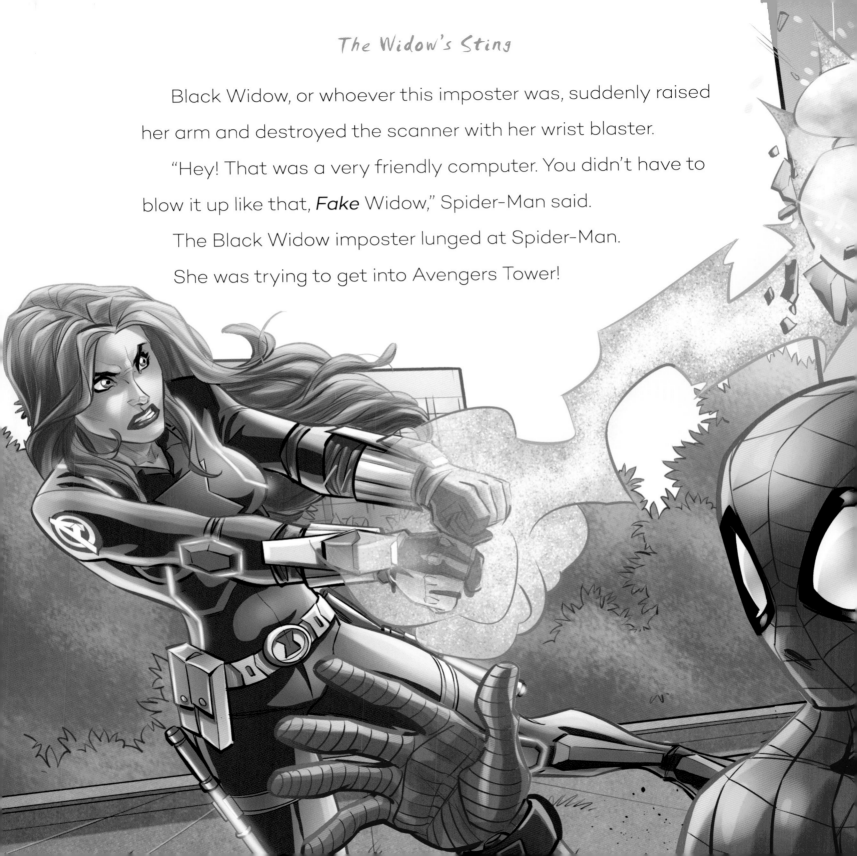

The Widow's Sting

Black Widow, or whoever this imposter was, suddenly raised her arm and destroyed the scanner with her wrist blaster.

"Hey! That was a very friendly computer. You didn't have to blow it up like that, *Fake* Widow," Spider-Man said.

The Black Widow imposter lunged at Spider-Man.

She was trying to get into Avengers Tower!

Spider-Man fired a web towards her, but the imposter vaulted through the air and landed gracefully on her feet behind him.

"Thanks for the ride," she said. "You even held the door for me. Such a gentleman." Black Widow ran towards the open door – only to have it slam in her face!

"I guess you're not on the guest list," Spider-Man said.

Frustrated, the false Black Widow blasted the doors, but they still didn't budge. "I don't think they're going to let you in," said Spider-Man.

As Spider-Man and the imposter began to fight, a familiar-looking shield blocked one of the blasts that was about to hit Spider-Man.

Another bolt of energy came shooting down from above, landing near the imposter's feet.

Looking up, Spider-Man saw two of his
Avengers friends coming to his aid: Captain
America and Iron Man!

With their help, Spider-Man continued to fight with the false Black Widow. She flipped and dodged Cap's shield as she fired her wrist blaster at Iron Man. "If only you had stepped aside and let me through, Spider-Fool."

"Sorry, rules are rules. I don't want to lose my guest pass," Spidey quipped, dodging one of the phony Widow's blasts.

Iron Man dived down, but the imposter was too fast, flipping over him and grabbing on to his back.

"You shouldn't give rides to strangers, Iron Man," the villain said.

Suddenly, Captain America's shield flew from behind and struck the imposter in the knees, knocking her to the ground with a thud.

Swinging into action, Spider-Man quickly webbed the evildoer's hands together, jamming the wrist blasters.

"I think it's time we find out who is behind the Black Widow mask," Spidey said.

Spider-Man pulled on the imposter's hair, but instead of a wig coming off in his hands, the foe's entire body changed! Where Black Widow had been, there now lay the pale-faced villain... the Chameleon!

The Chameleon was a master of disguise, and his suit gave him the ability to take on the form of anyone.

"I thought Black Widow was looking a little pale today," Spidey said.

"And you nearly fell for it, too," the Chameleon snarled.

As Iron Man flew away with the Chameleon, Spider-Man turned to Captain America. "I hope this doesn't mean I'm banned from Avengers Tower for life."

Cap laughed. "Spider-Man, if you hadn't made sure that imposter followed the rules, the Chameleon would have been able to sneak in. You're always welcome here, son."

Spidey was relieved. "Good, can we go inside now? Avengers Tower has the best video games and snacks in town."

MARVEL
SPIDER-MAN

Mysterio's Revenge

Thwip! Spider-Man shot a web across Fifth Avenue and swung past the Empire State Building. He was on his way towards the Daily Bugle. Peter Parker was late for work, and the only thing that could get him there in time were his web-shooters.

"Great," Peter said to himself as he fired another web. "If I'm late for work again, Mr. Jameson is going to explode!"

Just then, an explosion of green and purple smoke erupted from the top floor of the Daily Bugle building!

"Yikes! I didn't think he'd literally explode!" Spidey said. "Better get in there to see if anyone needs help."

Landing on the side of the building, Spider-Man crawled up the wall and looked through the window into the smoky office. That's when he heard a booming voice and his spider-sense started to tingle.

"Now that I have your attention," the bizarre voice began, "you will all witness the total destruction of the Daily Bugle!" Spider-Man recognised that voice – it was his enemy Mysterio, the master of illusion! The menacing Mysterio was holding J. Jonah Jameson by the tie and addressing the terrified staff.

"No one can help you now, Jameson, not even Spider-Man!" the villain hissed.

"That's my cue!" Spidey said as he launched himself at the villain. Spider-Man caught Mysterio by surprise, and the two tumbled to the ground, locked in combat!

As the Super Hero and Super Villain continued to fight, Jameson crawled to the exit.

He jiggled the doorknob frantically, but all the doors had been locked from the outside.

They were trapped!

"The Amazing Spider-Man!" Mysterio began.
"You're right on time... to meet your doom!"

Mysterio raised his arms and the newsroom filled with thick, green smoke. Then the villain disappeared into the fog right before everyone's eyes!

"Meet my doom?" Spider-Man said.
"What do you suppose he meant by that?"

Mysterio's voice echoed eerily across the room.

"Last I saw you, J. Jonah Jameson, you promised that you could deliver Spider-Man," the villain said. "Instead, I was defeated by Spider-Man... and now, you will all pay!" With that, Mysterio appeared through the smoke and lunged at J. Jonah Jameson.

Spider-Man knew he had to act fast! He fired a web and swung towards the villain. With unbelievable strength and speed, the Amazing Spider-Man kicked Mysterio in the chest and then fired another web at Jameson, sticking him to the wall.

"Sorry to disappoint you, Mysterio, but I don't have plans to meet my doom for at least another sixty or seventy years!" Spidey said.

Spider-Man stood above the trapped Mysterio and removed the villain's glass helmet. But Spidey was shocked at the person he saw beneath the mask: it was Peter Parker!

"Parker!" Jameson yelled. "You're Mysterio?!"

Mysterio was a master of disguise, but only Spider-Man knew that the villain wasn't really Peter Parker. *This must've been the disguise he was going to use in order to escape*, Spidey thought.

But how was Spider-Man going to save everyone in the Daily Bugle and prove that Mysterio wasn't Peter?

While all these thoughts ran through Spidey's mind, the villain leapt forward and attacked!

Ow, I hit hard! Spidey thought. As he tried to pick himself up off the floor, Mysterio delivered another hard blow. *I can't believe I'm beating myself up!* Spider-Man was dazed, but he rolled across the smoky room.

With Mysterio distracted by his precious helmet, Spidey looked around the office and realised the only person who wasn't there was the real Peter Parker.

That's why Mysterio used him for his disguise! And that gave the wall-crawler an idea.

Spidey jumped across the room and crawled along the wall, completely hidden by the smoke. He grabbed a hoodie off a desk, zipped it up to cover his suit and removed his mask.

Now it looked like the real Peter Parker had shown up. "Hey, guys. Sorry I'm late."

Mysterio turned, enraged. "No! How did you get in?"

"*Two* Parkers?" Jameson said, confused. "Next there will be *two* Spider-Men!"

"Not if I have anything to say about it!" Mysterio said. The appearance of the real Peter Parker had worked. While everyone was distracted, Peter ducked beneath the smoke, put his mask back on and charged at Mysterio.

Firing both web-shooters again and again, the Amazing Spider-Man captured Mysterio in a giant spiderweb for all to see.

Then, with a CRASH, the police finally broke into the newsroom, just as Spider-Man jumped out the nearest window. "Here you go, boys," Spidey said to the cops as he swung away.

"One gift-wrapped Super Villain, courtesy of you-know-who!"

A few minutes later, the real Peter Parker entered the newsroom. J. Jonah Jameson, who was still stuck to the side of the wall, looked down at him. "Parker," Jameson said, "you're late!" Peter sighed. It was just another day at the office for Peter Parker... and your friendly neighbourhood Spider-Man!

MARVEL

SPIDER-MAN

The Swashbuckling Spider

It was a good day to be Spider-Man. Earlier that morning, he had captured both Doctor Octopus and Sandman. Now, as the sun set, Spider-Man arrived at Avengers Tower. Nick Fury was there to greet him.

"Thanks for volunteering to keep an eye on the place while the Avengers are away," Nick said.

Spider-Man replied, with a firm handshake, "Not only will I keep one eye on the place, I'll keep two!"

Spider-Man hoped that if he did this favour for the Avengers, they might let him join their team someday. Before Nick Fury left, he gave Spider-Man one important instruction: watch the security monitors.

"Don't worry, I've got this," Spider-Man said confidently.

But watching the monitors was dull. So Spider-Man decided to do some exploring. His first stop was Tony Stark's lab. Inside, Spidey found a scroll that looked like a pirate's treasure map. But the scroll was covered in strange symbols. A note below the scroll read, 'HANDS OFF!'

69

Spidey knew he shouldn't touch the map. The last time he fiddled around with mysterious artifacts in Tony's lab, he got sent back in time to the Old West. But his curiosity got the better of him! He held the map up to the light and saw glistening circuitry and bizarre icons woven throughout the parchment.

Without thinking, Spider-Man tapped one of the icons. An enormous portal opened up – and sucked the web-slinger right into it.

"Whoaaa! Not again!" Spidey shouted as he plunged deeper down the portal.

Dazed, Spidey realised he was being tied up by a huge, hairy man. The man grabbed the wall-crawler, yanking him forwards.

"'Tis a masked scurvy dog who appeared out o' nowhere, sir!" the man growled. A massive buccaneer with a braided beard turned to look at Spider-Man. It was Blackbeard the pirate!

"Oh, hello, Blackbeard, the most notorious pirate who ever lived," Spider-Man quipped. "I would love to stay and chat, but I better get going." Spider-Man attempted to flee, but the legendary pirate was not going to let Spider-Man go so easily.

Blackbeard eyed the map in Spidey's pocket. Thinking it was a treasure map, the pirate king snatched it. Then he shoved Spider-Man onto a wooden plank that jutted out over the waves. The web-slinger bumped into a man with a hook for a hand, who was already standing at the edge of the plank. "I guess we're plankmates," Spidey joked to the man, who spun around to face him. It was Nick Fury!

But Spider-Man quickly realised that this wasn't actually Nick Fury. Nick had once told Spider-Man a story about his ancestor.

"You're 'One-Eyed' Fury!" Spider-Man said. "You're that English spy. Man, I thought Nick was pulling my leg."

"Will you keep your voice down, sir!" One-Eyed Fury said in a loud whisper. "I'm undercover."

"How's that working out for you so far?" Spidey asked.

But before they could chat any further, Blackbeard knocked Fury and Spidey overboard!

Thinking quickly, Spidey used his super-strength to break through his bonds. Then he shot his webs and swung over the water, catching Fury in mid-air. Both of them were now safely on deck... or so they thought. Spider-Man was untying Fury's ropes when Blackbeard's crew charged at them.

"Don't worry, I've got this." Spidey smirked, swiping Fury's hat. "Oh, and may I? I love a good costume!"

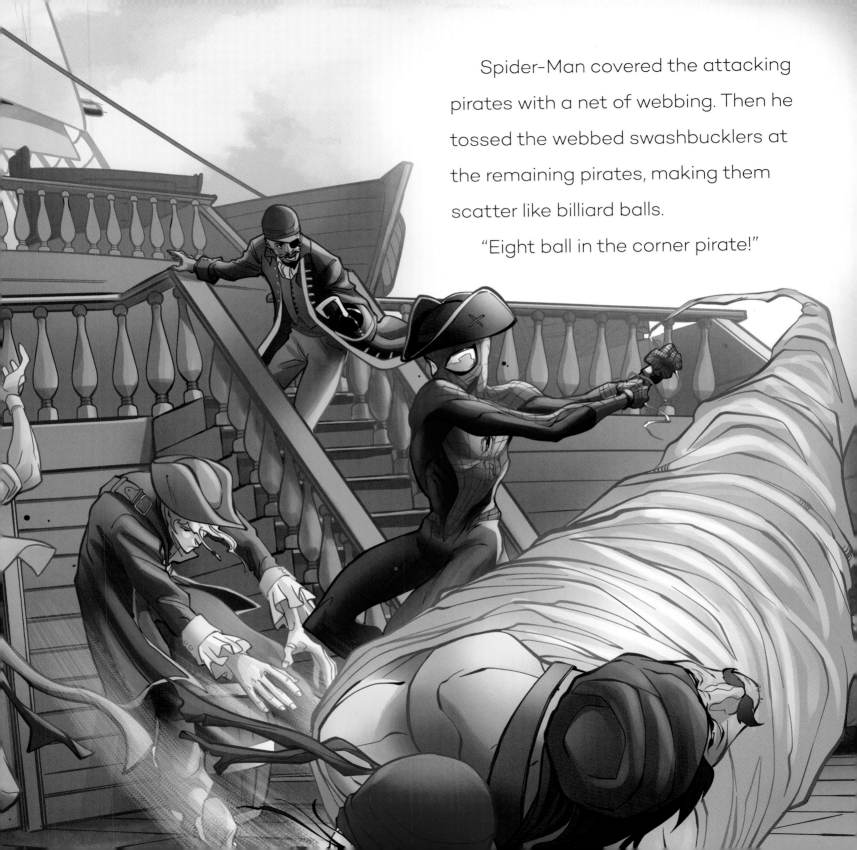

Spider-Man covered the attacking pirates with a net of webbing. Then he tossed the webbed swashbucklers at the remaining pirates, making them scatter like billiard balls.

"Eight ball in the corner pirate!"

Suddenly, Blackbeard snapped his

fingers and two ferocious female buccaneers appeared. "Ahoy, scallywags!

May I introduce ye to me buckos Sandy Dunes 'n' Doctor Squidlegs,"

Blackbeard boomed. "Ladies, attack!"

Spidey turned to One-Eyed Fury. "I can't understand a word this guy says."

Doctor Squidlegs's mechanical tentacles hissed and clicked as they came down all around Spider-Man and One-Eyed Fury, while Sandy Dunes whipped up a huge sandstorm. But Spider-Man and One-Eyed Fury were ready! The two heroes worked together as a team to take on the villains.

"Follow my lead, Fury!" Spider-Man shouted as he covered Doctor Squidlegs in webs.

"Is that all you got?" One-Eyed Fury asked. "Watch this!" The spy pressed a button on his sleeve and his hook hand transformed into a water cannon. A jet of water sprayed out of the cannon, melting Sandy Dunes!

Suddenly, the deck began to shake. Blackbeard had used the map to open a portal! Thinking quickly, One-Eyed Fury used his water cannon to pummel the famous pirate and his comrades, knocking them out cold.

"Not bad for a guy with one eye... and one hand," Spider-Man said as he grabbed the map and jumped through the portal.

"Thank you, sir!" One-Eyed Fury called out as he took control of the ship. "I hope we meet again!" As Spider-Man entered the portal, he could've sworn he saw something else fly through the portal with him.

The portal dropped Spider-Man back in the present day.

That was so much fun! Way more fun than watching monitors...

oh no! The monitors! Spidey rushed back to make sure nothing bad

had happened while he was gone. Everything looked quiet enough,

except for a flash of movement on one screen. It was Blackbeard's

parrot, and Spider-Man had to catch the feathered felon before it

wrecked all the furniture in Avengers Tower!

MARVEL
SPIDER-MAN
The Hunt for Black Panther

Kraven the Hunter loved to hunt wild animals. The only thing he loved more than hunting was the fame that came along with it. But one day, after Kraven had captured a pair of cheetahs, he didn't feel the same sense of accomplishment he normally felt after a successful hunt.

Kraven hungered for a new prey that would give him a real challenge.

But where could he find such a foe?

A few days later, Peter Parker was sent by the *Daily Bugle* to photograph the annual Protection of Endangered Animals conference in Upper Manhattan. Giving the keynote speech was none other than T'Challa, ruler of the African nation of Wakanda.

Peter was excited for the chance to actually see T'Challa speak. The king was a compassionate ruler and a scientific genius.

But T'Challa had a secret. He was also the Super Hero Black Panther!

"In order to protect the animals of Earth," the king began, "it is our duty to fight back against illegal hunters and poachers."

Black Panther protected his nation and its animal kingdom from villains by using his superhuman strength, speed and agility. One of those villains was Kraven the Hunter.

Desperate for a new challenge, Kraven knew that this conference was the perfect place to find his next prey – Black Panther! The villain burst through the window in a spray of broken glass.

"T'Challa!" he bellowed. "I request a meeting with the Black Panther."

T'Challa's eyes narrowed. "Black Panther will never bow to the likes of you!"

Kraven smirked. "I assumed there would be some protest."

"Which is why I brought some backup!" Kraven shouted. Just then, Kraven let out a high-pitched whistle and two cheetahs leapt down from the window above! "No one here is allowed to leave until the Black Panther is mine!"

In the chaos, Peter Parker's spider-senses were tingling like crazy. He knew he had to act fast. This place was turning into a zoo!

Meanwhile, T'Challa's bodyguards, the Dora Milaje, attempted to move the Wakandan king to safety.

"Save your energy," he commanded. "It's time for Black Panther to strike."

Black Panther turned round to discover he had been joined by Spider-Man!

"What are you doing here?" Black Panther asked.

"Nice to see you, too," Spider-Man said as he fired a ball of web fluid at the nearest cheetah. "Stand back – I've beaten Kraven before. I can deal with these overgrown house cats."

"Spider-Man, no! You must be careful!" Black Panther tried to warn the web-slinger, but it was already too late.

"Whoa! Nice kitty!" Spider-Man exclaimed as the cheetah grabbed his web and lunged towards him.

Acting fast, Black Panther grabbed the cheetah before Spider-Man was harmed.

"Listen to me. My animal instincts tell me that these creatures are being held here against their will. They will only attack you if they are provoked."

But Spidey wasn't out of danger yet! Kraven threw a spear at the web-slinger, but Spidey rolled out of the way just in time!

"I'll calm them down while you get Kraven," Black Panther said to Spidey.

"On it!" Spider-Man said as he swung towards the balcony.

Black Panther massaged the backs of the cheetahs' heads, safely pressing down on their pressure points to relax the animals' anger.

"That should calm you down," he said, petting the cheetahs.

With the cheetahs under control, Spider-Man caught up with the villainous hunter, who began throwing knives at the web-slinging hero. Unfortunately for Kraven, Spidey's trusty spider-sense made it impossible for him to land an attack.

"What's the matter, Kraven?" Spider-Man asked. "Can't catch a little spider?"

"Maybe it would help if you took care of that smell first, Kraven. P-U! Or do they not have showers in the jungle?" Spider-Man joked.

Blinded with anger, Kraven was unable to focus on the fight with the two Super Heroes. Spider-Man quickly used his web-shooters to disarm Kraven, giving Black Panther the perfect opening for an attack.

"Now you will pay for the crimes you have committed against the animal kingdom!" Black Panther added, before delivering the final blow to Kraven. The hunter was clearly no match for the strength and speed of the King of Wakanda.

Kraven was finally defeated.

"Beaten by a spider and a cat," Kraven mumbled.

"What's wrong? Don't like being held in captivity?" Spider-Man asked.

Black Panther addressed the crowd of frightened spectators. "You are all safe! These majestic creatures are not the enemy. They deserve respect and compassion. And thank you, Spider-Man, for helping me save them."

Spider-Man was caught off guard by the Black Panther's kind words. "Wow. Thanks, Black Panther. Now might not be a good time, but do you mind if we take a selfie?"

Seeing Spots

It was a wonderfully sunny day. Peter Parker and Gwen Stacy were strolling through Central Park, about to buy hot dogs from a vending cart. "Ketchup, mustard and relish?" Peter asked.

"You know me too well, Parker," Gwen said, smiling.

Peter reached into his pocket to pay for the hot dogs when Gwen reached for her purse. "My treat," she said.

Before Peter could argue, a strange black circle appeared below Gwen's purse. The friends were shocked when a white arm covered in black spots came shooting out of the hole. It grabbed Gwen's purse! Another circle appeared above them. Inside, a man's head appeared.

A menacing voice erupted from the circle. "What a lovely bag. I'm sorry, but I don't believe there will be any hot dogs today."

As suddenly as they appeared, the thief and his black circles disappeared. Gwen was shocked. Peter's eyes narrowed. He was not going to let some freaky villain ruin his perfect day with Gwen.

"Wait here!" Peter exclaimed. Before Gwen could say anything, Peter bolted out of sight.

Peter ducked into an alley and changed into his Spider-Man suit to chase down the thief. He was a robber called the Spot! Swinging high, Spider-Man looked out over the streets of New York for signs of the criminal.

"Ha! I *spot* you!" he chuckled as he saw black circles appear beside another potential victim.

He swung off to face his foe.

Spider-Man managed to web the purse before the Spot could snatch it.

"Spider-Man! I've been waiting to run into you," the Spot said. "Over and over."

Suddenly, black circles appeared all around Spidey. Out of them came fists, hitting Spider-Man as the Spot appeared and reappeared in different directions. The villain was so fast that even Spider-Man's spider-sense couldn't keep up.

Spider-Man fell, beaten by the Spot. The teleporting villain appeared over him, laughing.

"Better luck next time, Bug-Brain!" the Spot taunted, vanishing into thin air.

Feeling woozy, Spidey realised he was going to need some help defeating this new menace.

Fortunately, he knew just who to call.

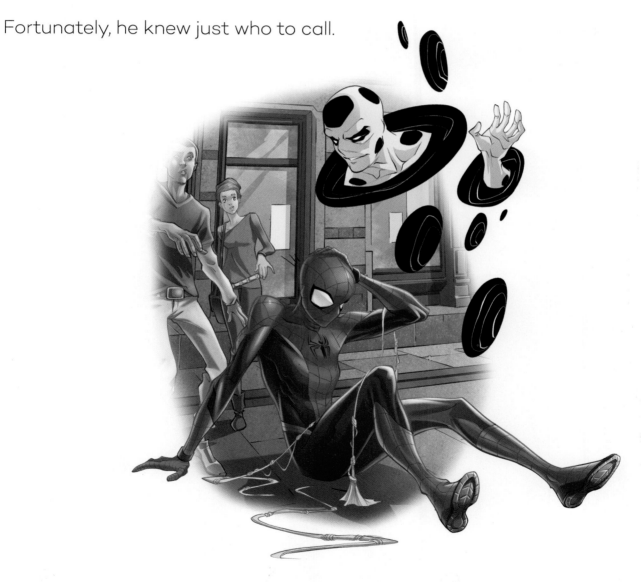

Spidey swung to an abandoned church, hoping this was still the place his friends used as a hideout.

"If anyone can help me, it'll be these two," he muttered, knowing he was running out of options. The Spot was going to be hard to defeat.

Although they had only teamed up a few times before, and one of the two could be kind of creepy, Spider-Man knew he could trust this duo to help him get the job done.

"Cloak! Dagger! Man, am I glad to see you guys," Spider-Man said as he entered the church. He quickly filled them in on his encounter with the Spot.

"I need your help." Spidey turned to Cloak. "I know you're used to popping in and out of thin air, too."

"I have felt someone tapping into my teleportation force recently," Cloak noted. "It seems this Spot and I share a connection through multiple dimensions."

That gave Dagger an idea. "If we can follow the energy Cloak is feeling, it could lead us to the Spot. Then my light daggers could help trap him there by draining his energy."

With the plan set, the heroes dived into the darkness of Cloak's cape and disappeared.

When the trio reappeared, they found themselves in the Spot's secret hideout. It was filled with all the stolen purses, jewels and other items the thief had taken on his crime spree.

"Spider-Man! How did you find me here? And who are these freaks?" the Spot asked, shocked.

Spider-Man just smiled. "Looks like you're not the only disappearing act in town, Spot."

The Spot tore the teleporting discs off of his suit, threw them around the room, and started to dive into them. He was ready to attack! But this time, the good guys were ready, too.

Bright knives shot out of Dagger's hands and burst into the dark circles. Her illuminating power filled the darkness in which the Spot thrived. They pushed out the Spot, cutting off his escape.

Spider-Man quickly webbed the villain before he could try his teleportation tricks again. "Hmm, looks like you're stuck. I guess you could say my webs are *spot-* on!"

Dagger chuckled at Spider-Man's bad joke, while Cloak's icy stare never wavered. Their plan worked!

The Spot's thieving days were over.

The heroes helped return the stolen items. As the pile grew smaller, Spidey recognised one of the purses and grabbed it.

"Not enough pockets in your suit?" Dagger asked with a wink.

"Hey, bad jokes are my thing," Spider-Man replied.

Then with a quiet whoosh, Cloak whisked Dagger and the Spot away.

Back in Central Park, Peter Parker came running back to Gwen. There was a police officer handing over her purse.

"Gwen! You got it back!" Peter exclaimed.

"It was incredible, Peter! Spider-Man caught the thief and brought all the stolen items back. Including my purse."

Peter blushed. "Wow, he's a real hero."

"But you are just as brave, Peter," Gwen said, hugging her friend. "Thanks for looking out for me."

Peter grinned. "I'm sorry I couldn't do more."

"Well," Gwen said, handing the hot dog vendor money, "you certainly did enough to earn this hot dog. My treat, as promised."

"You're the best," Peter said as he chewed. "Wow, this really hits the *spot*."

The Amazing Incredible Spider-Hulk

Spider-Man and the Avengers were having dinner at a restaurant after they battled Ultron in Central Park. When they'd finished and headed outside, Spider-Man watched as a little girl shyly tugged at the Hulk's trouser leg. "Excuse me," she mumbled. "Will you sign my autograph book?"

The Hulk nodded, but when he grabbed the pencil, he accidentally crushed it. Spidey could see his friend was upset.

The Hulk told him he wanted to be, as he put it, "more puny, like Bug-Man."

"Isn't that something," Spider-Man began. "Sometimes I'd rather be more like you!" Just then, they received an important message. Nick Fury was unveiling an important new invention!

At S.H.I.E.L.D. headquarters, Nick Fury was standing next to a device capped by an enormous purple gemstone. Fury explained that the machine would allow two Super Heroes to temporarily swap abilities.

Spidey and the Hulk were very excited. It would be like switching places! When Fury asked for volunteers, two hands immediately went up.

Project A.S.S.E.M.B.L.E.
Ability Switching and
Super-power Exchange
Mighty Big Laser Engine.

Spider-Man and the Hulk stood side by side over a big red X on the floor. Fury activated the device. The machine started to hum and the purple gemstone glowed. It shot out a beam, covering both the Hulk and Spider-Man.

But the machine overheated, causing an explosion that shook the room! When the smoke cleared, everyone stared at the figure standing on the red **X**. It wasn't Spidey. It wasn't the Hulk.

It looked like both of them... combined! Two heroes had merged into one hybrid creature...

The Spider-Hulk!

Peering at Iron Man's armour, Spider-Hulk studied his reflection in its gleaming surface. The face that stared back at him was familiar, and yet... unfamiliar.

Confused and frustrated, Spider-Hulk couldn't control his feelings.

"Bug-Hulk SMASH!" he yelled, pounding his fists into the floor.

Captain America tried to calm down the heroic hybrid, but Spider-Hulk grabbed Cap's shield and flung it into the wall. Then the frightened Spider-Hulk turned and crashed through the glass window. The Avengers raced after him.

Spider-Hulk couldn't think clearly. It felt as though there were two separate voices in his head! He just wanted to get away from the people trying to capture him. He didn't realise his pursuers were his friends, the Avengers.

"Bug-Hulk's bug-sense tingling," he muttered to himself.

Spider-Hulk tried using his webbing to outrun the Avengers, but when he attempted to swing away, his body twisted awkwardly in the air. The web-line snapped and Spider-Hulk fell, smashing into the pavement below!

With Spider-Hulk momentarily weakened, Hawkeye quickly came up with a plan. He had sometimes calmed the Hulk down with a nursery rhyme, so he sat down and began reading to Spider-Hulk. It worked too well. The hybrid hero thought it was bedtime and he fled looking for a midnight snack!

This gave Black Widow an idea. The Avengers would draw Spider-Hulk back to S.H.I.E.L.D. headquarters using the one thing both Spider-Man and the Hulk love: food! When Thor and Black Widow found Spider-Hulk, he was ransacking every hot dog cart in the city looking for snacks. Thor stood in his path and tried to lure Spider-Hulk away with a delicious chocolate cake from the bakery.

But before Thor could lead the way back to headquarters, Spider-Hulk swallowed the entire cake. The new Super Hero also had a super appetite!

Iron Man knew that Spider-Man was really Peter Parker, a teenager who couldn't resist his Aunt May's famous wheat cakes. So the armoured Avenger instructed his personal chef to make enough wheat cakes to feed a small country. In other words, enough wheat cakes to feed one Spider-Hulk.

Iron Man zoomed around the city, leaving a trail of wheat cakes for his fused friend to follow. It worked! The Spider-Hulk gobbled each tasty treat, leading him closer and closer to the device that caused all this chaos in the first place.

Spider-Hulk was so busy wolfing down wheat cakes that he didn't notice he was sitting on the big red X. He swallowed the last piece of wheat cake and said, "Spider-Hulk wants maple—"

But before he could finish his sentence, Nick Fury pressed the reverse button.

Once again the purple gemstone glowed and Spider-Hulk was shot with an energy beam. When the light faded, two heroes stepped forth: Spider-Man and the Hulk!

"I really learnt something today," Spider-Man told the Hulk. "I used to think I wanted to be more like you. But being Spider-Hulk just... didn't feel like me. And I like being me."

The green goliath nodded. "Hulk learnt something, too," he began. "Hulk learnt that Bug-Man's puny costume is bad fit on Hulk-size body!"

The two friends laughed. Then they patted their bellies and turned to the other Avengers.

"Okay," Spider-Man said with a wink, "who's up for some dessert?"

MARVEL
SPIDER-MAN

Mega Meltdown

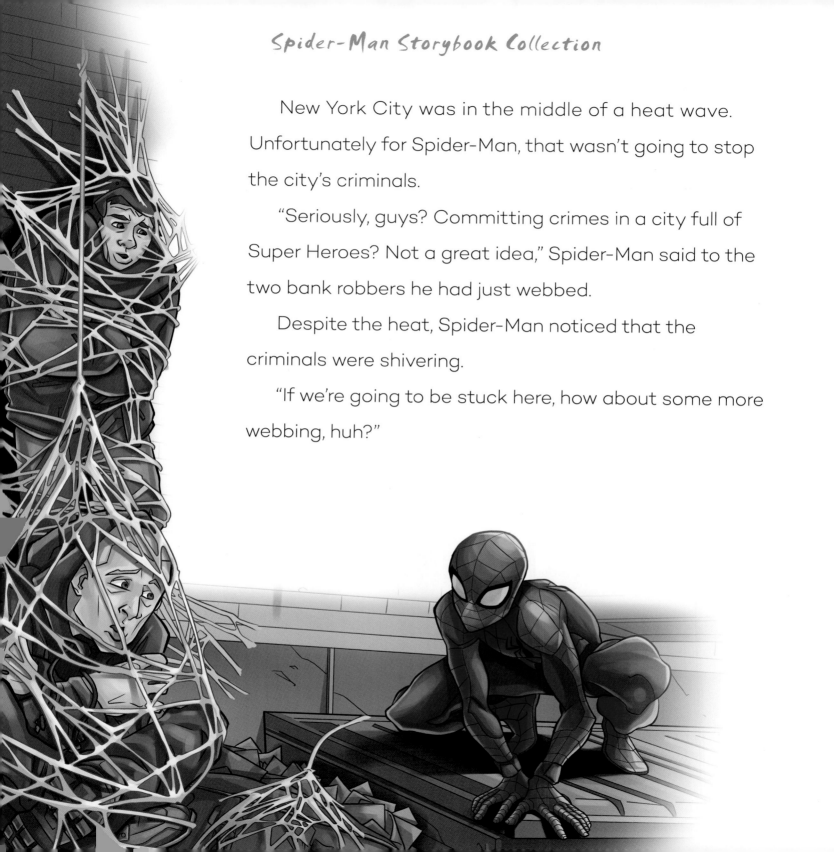

New York City was in the middle of a heat wave. Unfortunately for Spider-Man, that wasn't going to stop the city's criminals.

"Seriously, guys? Committing crimes in a city full of Super Heroes? Not a great idea," Spider-Man said to the two bank robbers he had just webbed.

Despite the heat, Spider-Man noticed that the criminals were shivering.

"If we're going to be stuck here, how about some more webbing, huh?"

Mega Meltdown

Why were those guys acting like it's cold? Spider-Man thought as he swung away. *It's been a scorcher for weeks!*

As he swung closer to Times Square, Spider-Man's spider-sense began to tingle. The wind started to whip around him as the temperature steadily dropped.

Maybe it is a little chilly today.

Just then, Spider-Man came across the source of the changing weather. A gigantic portal had opened up in the sky, sending snow flurries down upon the city.

Loki, the trickster god of Asgard, was standing on a skyscraper clutching a Cosmic Cube!

Spider-Man swung down to confront the Super Villain. "Ah, the Spider. I invite you to witness the start of my glorious reign," Loki said proudly.

"Yeah, right," Spider-Man said. "What are a few snowflakes going to do?"

"Just wait until you meet my friends," Loki cackled.

Suddenly, a group of Frost Giants leapt from the portal! Parked cars were crushed under the weight of the massive giants as they lumbered through the streets. Frightened tourists ran for cover as sparks from collapsing billboards rained down upon them. "Meet the Frost Giants of Jotunheim," Loki said in an otherworldly voice. "Now that I have the Cosmic Cube, they are under my control!"

Spider-Man knew there was only one thing to do.

He leapt into action.

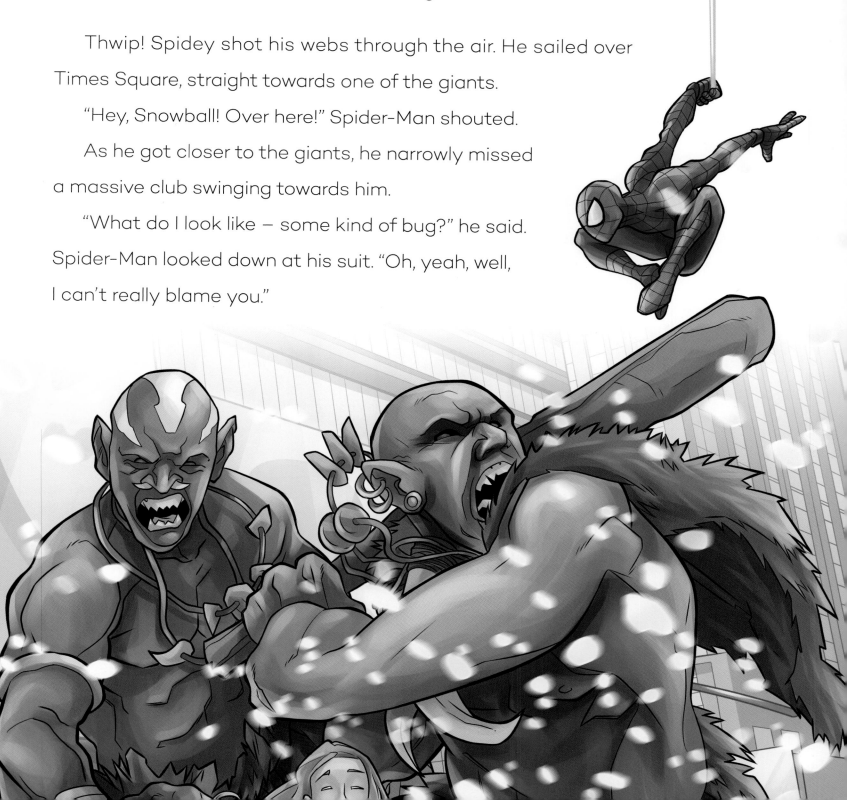

Thwip! Spidey shot his webs through the air. He sailed over Times Square, straight towards one of the giants.

"Hey, Snowball! Over here!" Spider-Man shouted.

As he got closer to the giants, he narrowly missed a massive club swinging towards him.

"What do I look like – some kind of bug?" he said. Spider-Man looked down at his suit. "Oh, yeah, well, I can't really blame you."

Spider-Man swung out of reach, then approached the Frost Giants once more. The mindless giants paid him no attention. They were only concerned with one thing: destruction.

I don't have enough webbing left to tie up Frosty and friends, Spidey thought. *But this should slow them down.*

Spider-Man fired a web across the street. He hoped this barrier would stop the Frost Giants' march.

It looked like the Frost Giants were finally going to be stopped when... BOOM! Spider-Man was shocked to witness the Frost Giants step on his web barrier, causing two billboards to crash to the ground.

Just then, Spider-Man spotted an Avengers Quinjet flying over.

"It's about time!" Spidey exclaimed. He knew that with friends like Captain America, Thor, Black Widow and Iron Man on his side, Loki and his snow buddies didn't stand a chance!

Spider-Man approached the jet as it landed on a nearby rooftop. As the cargo ramp lowered, Spider-Man saw only one hero. One very small hero.

"So, what's the situation here?"

"Ant-Man?!" Spider-Man was shocked as the miniature hero walked down the ramp. "Where's everyone else?"

"The Avengers are busy with Thanos," Ant-Man said. "That guy never takes a day off. Nick Fury called and said there was some trouble in the city. I'm here to back you up, pal."

"No offence, but I was expecting some bigger guns," Spider-Man said. "How are two bugs going to stop three giants?"

"Well, looks like these 'two bugs' are all New York has today."

Spider-Man knew Ant-Man was right. Two heads were better than one. And with that, Ant-Man grabbed on to Spidey's suit as he swung back towards the wintry chaos.

As soon as Spider-Man
and Ant-Man rejoined the Frost Giants,
one of them threw a car at the two heroes.

"Look out!" Ant-Man exclaimed.

"Way ahead of you!" Spider-Man responded as he
swiftly dodged the car. "But this heavy snowfall isn't making
anything easier! Any ideas?"

"Well, if they want to head to Central Park, I can send in some ants
to ruin their picnic," Ant-Man said sarcastically.

"Even so, it's not warm enough for a picnic," Spider-Man said. "But wait! That gives me an idea! How much do you know about electricity?"

"More than you, kid," Ant-Man said. "And I think I know where you're going with this."

Evading attacks from Loki's Frost Giants, Spidey swung towards Times Tower, the brightest building in the city.

Mega Meltdown

As Spider-Man approached the tower, Ant-Man was able to jump just before a Frost Giant grabbed Spider-Man's webbing. The giant pulled the webs, yanking him off of the tower.

"Oomph!" Spider-Man exclaimed as he crashed onto the hard cement.

Ant-Man knew Spider-Man couldn't hold back the giants for long. He squeezed between the bright billboards. Once inside, the small hero was able to hack into the main power grid.

"Hey, you big bullies!" Ant-Man shouted. "How about turning up the heat!"

Suddenly, Times Square began to brighten. The lights became brighter and brighter until the light from the billboards was blinding. Hit with 161 megawatts of power, the Frost Giants quickly began to shrink until they vanished completely.

"It's working!" Spider-Man said as he swung to face Loki. "Looks like your Frost Giants should've brought some sun cream."

"Spider-Man!" Loki roared. "You did this?" Spider-Man quickly shot a web straight towards Loki. "I had some help. Not too bad for a couple of bugs, huh?"

With Loki blinded by webbing, Spider-Man was able to take the Cosmic Cube out of his grasp. Using the power of the Cosmic Cube, Spider-Man opened up a portal and sent Loki back to Jotunheim.

"I'll be back, Spider – I always come back!" Loki screamed as he was pulled into the portal at high speed.

"Defeated Loki, melted a bunch of Frost Giants and caused a blackout in Times Square," Ant-Man said. "Man, we deserve a holiday."

"You're right," Spider-Man responded. "But we still have to return this cube and restore power to Times Square."

"Yeah, but first... Spider! My ants and I challenge thee to a snowball fight!" Ant-Man said, mocking Loki.

"You're on!"

The End